THE CYCLE OF CYRNOS

THE CYCLE OF CYRNOS

Book One: Origins

By Pascal Paul Piazza

ISBN: 9781980892373

TABLE OF CONTENTS

CHAPTER ONE

The Roman Duet of Hyperboleum and Delerium Ponders on History
Unearthed and Unknown

HYPERBOLEUM

We sing to praise a woman and a man
who by acts tempt their fate and show they can
with spiral pith and path cross the Great Sea
to name the isle of beauty, conch and fee.

DELERIUM

We did not think a search for a small plant
would cause much more than a curt cavil rant.
Yet, the spirals where we sit and you sit
heard the words become myth seeding great wit.

HYPERBOLEUM

The myth became wedges on a clay pot
known to Sumer's priests, kings and lower lot.
It is now unknown, but for broken shards
strewn about time, sand, dust and shifting yards.

DELERIUM

The shards now rest as one puzzle to solve
by a scholar and daughter with resolve,
but derailed by gaps and sanded wedge text
not knowing what could be or not done next.

HYPERBOLEUM

Is there a history where there are gaps
among wedges, forms and such etched maps?
Yes, send magic, muse and a mind to draw
and walk again and to see what they once saw!

The Magician En (a/k/a Lug) and Lil (a/k/a Al) is a Cat (who Talks) Visit Mary and Her Daughter Charlotte (and who is not a spider)

LIL

"Which of these doors of cool metallic white
which easily may be out of keen sight
which are lost in a plastic mottled floor
and which hide Mary behind a blank door?

EN

"Mary was often like her portal;
looking to be lost behind her chortle.
A genius, but with ginger hair to tame
A crystal clear mind, but an opaque name."

LIL

"The door opens to tablets of dry clay
of broken wedges aligned by an array
of dust, lines and order of each die cast --
a freeze-frame scene of hard history past."

MARY

"Who are you who burst open my door,
but I really do not care much any more
unless your name is Kramer or Skaggs,
Charlotte, please help sort out the bags."

LIL

"I would think a cat that talks is news
rather than an old mentor or old clues.
There is a key to the epic protean tale
that these cut wedges just want to tell."

3

CHARLOTTE

"Do not put before us some fictive tease.
We can read the words too if you so please,
but as broken lines meet the sanded text;
no words jump in to fill empty space next."

MARY

"My daughter, be patient and we will rest
and hear what this cat says to us in geste
or with a precise compass scale and seal
reveals the secret of this mason's deal."

LIL

"My cat eyes spy each word on a dull pad
and the tracks of tears that make you so mad.
Can France and Sumer be so tightly bound?
No one will believe the answer you found."

CHARLOTTE

"Mother, what is this new feline riddle?
What can it mean in the edge or middle?
Show me what I need to have and to know.
O silence, select for me seeds to sow."

NARRATOR

Lil purred as En took Mary's left hand.
Mary read aloud unbroken words so grand
that they charmed space and speed to stop
and all in the room slept as time did drop.

CHAPTER TWO

The Roman Quartet of Hyperboleum, Delerium
Mary and Charlotte Ask Where Did We Go When the Rains Came

HYPERBOLEUM

"Come sit now and watch from this our far perch.
You too will find answers to your long search.
The rains make a mist so we can each see
a wedge turn, twist and now come to be."

DELERIUM

"There are no gaps or breaks in this live tale
on lost tablets found in that sandy tell.
The story pulsates like no stylus can etch
It is a canvass and a breathing sketch."

HYPERBOLEUM

"Do you know what land it is that we view?
Does the dance of ice and grass give a clue?
Do you have courage to say what is right?
Even when eyes and dogma are in a fight?"

MARY

"Charlotte and I can tell you this is France
when it was a refuge from the cold trance
of ice and snow consuming the firm ground
and before the Younger Dryas came round."

DELERIUM

"Well done, as you were not so firm and sure
what was in this text that was a main lure
to tie west to east when you were long taught
that such ideas are wrong and should be fought."

Cor Hunts in the Massif Central in the
Mesolithic Before the Onset of the Younger Dryas

NARRATOR

Cor knew the land like the back of his hand.
He had walked it alone and with his band.
He could smell the sweet grass along a trail;
food for the cattle plodding tail-by-tail.

NARRATOR

He too had his far perch where he could see
and decide which plump prey that day would be
food for the village and bones for the tools
and a blood offer for each god which still rules.

NARRATOR

He caressed the leaf-like stone point and edge
made from his own chert outcrop on a ledge
above his cave home but out of plain sight
each felt flake infused him with equal might.

NARRATOR

He and his band had traveled far in boats
next to the great Ice Arc where snow still floats.
He hunted, fished and left points in a land
green and un-touched by any other band.

NARRATOR

It was here at home that made Cor now blush
and prepare in time and space for the rush
to be made by horse, ibex, ox or deer
hungry for sprouts and grain not used for beer.

Narrator

Cor tracked the moon in each shape and size
with a bone burl notch on a stone that ties
the wind, rain, and cold with a prey's prance.
He would not leave the hunt subject to chance.

Narrator

He felt the tenth notch made by antler bone
which took the shape of a quarter moon cone.
It told him it was time to hunt the prey,
but there were no herds to be seen this day.

Narrator

His eye saw the signs for prey to be there,
but the sight of any herd is now rare.
There is a design that should make a sound
luring prey, but silence covers the ground.

Narrator

The cold grips and tightens his hairless face;
an un-healed leg bone slows his return pace.
He needs some answer before he walks back
to explain why things are not yet on track.

Narrator

When young, he had many questions to ask
there were no elders there up to this task.
He found his answers in a cave so dark
where there lived an ibex with an x-mark.

NARRATOR

Hungry and tired, Cor went to that cave
where before the ibex alone did save
his cloudy mind showing nature in a sane
array of prey, men and seed on one plain.

NARRATOR

Cor then slept alone on a cold bed slate;
he fell quickly into a warm dream state.
Then there was a tap, tap, tap of a hoof
with light and dark together on the roof.

IBEX

"Look, the brown ochre horses on the wall
and the geese and puffins there set to fall
are not caught in some rote cycle of stone
which they follow like a note does a tone."

IBEX

"There is a clue far from here that you seek
that will be a gift made by one so meek.
Walk long and far to find what you may be,
as you find the axis of the Great Sea."

NARRATOR

Before he could talk, he kept both eyes shut
so sleep could be the balm to solve the cut
of a path unknown, but with many a fold,
in a tale long to be told and re-told.

CHAPTER THREE

The Roman Quartet: Delerium, Hyperboleum, Mary and Charlotte Discuss Just How Far Mary and Charlotte Had Arrived

HYPERBOLEUM

"Do you know what gift the ibex fore-told?
Will it be a grail or a band of gold
born in the fire-forge at the dawn of time
each the subject of both prose and rhyme?"

MARY

"You speak of hubris and control of life
where cold mettle curtly is cut from strife.
We make stone walls and metal sheets of tin
yet we know that there is more than our ken."

DELERIUM

"No, it is a thing sprung forth from the dirt.
It is a hope and a salve for all hurt.
It shows that we are more correct than not.
It is a balm long lost and oft forgot."

HYPERBOLEUM

"The gift was found in the Garden long lost
next to the Tree and ignored at a cost.
It may be found when the ground is so cold
that ice is a kiss from the wind so bold."

DELERIUM

"It tells us there is much we still must learn.
What runs in a line might circle or turn.
Only a heart and mind of alloys pure
Will, after some travels, find the right cure."

NARRATOR

Cor slept until he could no longer sleep
just inside the mouth of the cave so steep.
He had to walk home to find his new path,
but first he wanted some food and a bath.

NARRATOR

Cor left the cave mouth as fast as he could
walking with the arc of the sun that would
soon start to sink with the length of the day
and pangs of want and need kept him at bay.

NARRATOR

Then he saw a meek girl with a blue hood
without a name, but who came with hot food.
He drew to smell the lentils and chick peas
she had made in a pot under the trees.

NARRATOR

Cor ran up, but she did not show any fear.
She did not speak, but bid him to come near
and fed him like a mother would a child
and he then slept again now in the wild.

NARRATOR

The mist of the new morn was a shower
that made him rise and find an odd flower
she had fit in his shirt as the one key
the ibex foretold that Cor would soon see.

Cor Encounters Volpe, the Shaman

NARRATOR

Cor stood up, but he did not really know
the power the young Dryas plant could show.
This plant and the ibex words were like a shell
with a twist and a curve telling the tale.

NARRATOR

Cor took ten steps when he met one he knew
in search of plants fresh with a misty dew.
Volpe looked up with each eye brow tight.
Fear cut hard, but there would be no flight.

VOLPE

"What flower is that you hold in your hand?
I know each root, seed or plant in our land.
I can heal with a salve made from a petal
or scare you to question your own mettle."

COR

"You know the moral from a trance so old,
but you have not seen the flower you hold.
The plant grows not in our place or our time.
This is a pilgrim far beyond the rime."

VOLPE

"I fear she that came and bore this gift
that you hope is a key, yet I feel is a rift.
You say it is a clue to find the herds,
but there is bile and not meat from the birds."

Volpe Goes into a Feigned Trance
With Tales of the Mythical Cat – the Ghjattu

NARRATOR

The two men did not wait as they went home.
Cor had to tell the elders he must roam.
The tribe then met as one above the dell
when Volpe went into a fit and fell.

NARRATOR

He spew and spit like badgers in a ball;
ashen black like the suet on the wall
of a cave where a flame frames a wraith
of charcoal for Volpe to keep the faith.

NARRATOR

A crack racks pain in each leg and a hand,
yet one eye is open to watch the band
react and tense to a fall and a cry
to his sulphur smile and his crazy eye.

VOLPE

"The Sun was midwife to life being born
before any path laid out for us was worn.
The Sun set the Moon to serve as a guide
for the rhyme and cycle of life in stride."

VOLPE

"The Moon phases so that it will be foretold
of green shifts that will give way to the cold.
Ghjattu is mad and growls against the Sun;
his body blocks all heat so life is undone."

NARRATOR

Cor let Volpe dance and squirm by a fire,
as he sat next to sparks from the pyre.
Cor did not think that a cat made the cold
to punish us for the hunt or acts bold.

NARRATOR

It was time to see the Forme close by,
who plan if it is wet, cold, warm or dry;
who work out details of each solution.
Surely, they would have some resolution.

NARRATOR

Cor put on a new cloth pant and a shirt.
If for a short time there would be no dirt.
He had an antler and shells on a string
with spirals, points, some food and a ring.

NARRATOR

A notch on the antler mimicked the moon.
Just two full phases would pass very soon
and he would finish the path so well worn
to be with his friends since he was first born.

NARRATOR

Cor also would stop along the short way
to find black glass or chert so he could pay
homage to his friends with a fine, thin tool
to help them hunt as the heat became cool.

CHAPTER FOUR

CHARLOTTE

"Should we read just that found within the text?
Is there a path in this line here and next?
Am I an ant duty-bound to the plot?
How can a void fill a missing bon mot?"

HYPERBOLEUM

"You read to impress, but still miss the mark.
Love, dreams and hope may be found in the dark.
A void has lines lost only now in stone.
You have more than just what you have alone."

DELERIUM

"Thirst for answers is like the need for salt.
Preserves the fresh and tempers the brew malt.
Wicks fear out of a breath from morn to dusk.
Encrusts words etched on stone or grey tusk."

HYPERBOLEUM

"Salt still can kill if we overlook the side
where harm so lurks to hinder and to hide.
It may take a tumble in a warming cave
to cleanse the grains spread out as a wave."

MARY

"These idle words hide that path to a field
where Cor finds Sica guiding the crop yield
before she earns a trip across the sea
so they can start the story that will be."

Cor Among the Forme

NARRATOR

The path south split the Sun's arc in the day
over hills, trees, a plain and stone which lay
open until rocks rise to cast the die
of a narrow pass door for prey to try.

NARRATOR

The words of intact grass spoke loud and long.
It was a harsh, shrill, callow and cold song
of lament and a call to herds on track
to return and funnel food and bone back.

NARRATOR

Cor did not stop long to fear or to muse.
Pangs of pain delayed thoughts of the ruse
that has upset the deer, ox and the fowl
to hide long time away with horse and owl.

NARRATOR

He could not wait to see Farru the chief
of the Forme and the source of relief
of geese, lentils, chick-pea and other food
and a welcome supply of stone and wood.

NARRATOR

His father's brother would open his home
and tell him why he did not need to roam.
Cor kept each eye open looking for tricks
that might lurk and wait among the dry sticks.

NARRATOR

Cor then saw what he had thought had been lost
It was a large ox erect in the frost.
Maybe the Sun-arc-sign was true and right.
There would be such a great feast had tonight,

NARRATOR

In the narrow entry, Cor had to be bold.
He was down-wind and even in the cold
his smell alone would cause the ox to run.
But, one quick blow might be the one to stun.

NARRATOR

Yet, the ox did not move despite his pace.
It stayed-put fetid in the same place.
He came face-to-face with a rotting head
on a pole supporting an ox long dead.

NARRATOR

Cor coughed, winced re-tracing his path.
He did not want to suffer the full wrath
of any tribe that scares others away
by such a sign-post beyond Nature's sway.

NARRATOR

Cor walked around this sentinel beast
which would not provide to him any feast.
Such a totem should surely be taboo,
But now he had to decide what to do.

Narrator

His steps stopped when a spear flew close by
Today, was not the day he chose to die.
A point hit the ox and then on the stone
He did not like his chances all alone.

Narrator and Farru

Farru jumped out and waved each hand.
"Stop, this is an old friend long to this land.
Enough, this is no wild, stalking beast.
Let us gather as one for a great feast."

Narrator and Farru

Farru hugs Cor and says, "Be of good cheer.
Yes, rest still among your blood ties here.
The ox should be feared by hearts so rife
with some static fear of the fulsome strife."

Farru

"We too read each full Moon and new Sun sign,
Yet the herds ignore the constant design.
What is the answer, I know not to boast
We just hope there is still meat to roast."

Cor

"You may be the hope that we all do seek.
Now is not the time to pause or be meek.
The cold taunts the Sun even in the day
Heat will die and leave during the fray."

FARRU

"We share this valley with a second tribe
who act with no formal rules to prescribe
what to eat, when to eat or how to eat.
Ice will be a force they cannot defeat."

ANCHISES

"Inside, we build, store and plan ahead
when the prey away from here are led.
Outside, they play and do not conserve.
They feel there is no need for a reserve."

FARRU

"We work in measure as we meet to plan.
We account for each one of the clan.
Work prevents idle and useless actions.
We band alike to avoid hard factions."

ANCHISES

"They live by right only to seize a day.
They do not care what the signs now say.
They hope for an invisible firm hand
to guide and gather food for the band."

FARRU

"They even deny that there will be a chill.
They only want to find more bags to fill.
To them, the cold is all just some big game
and they will soon master it just the same."

COR

"I will stay to help in the certain fight.
My hand can increase your right or might.
I have this flower for some new magic.
As one, we will prevent something tragic."

FARRU

"Your offer is true, but the plant must find
its own home among its own old kind.
The Akrida will boast and will complain,
but will reach an accord that will not wane."

ANCHISES

"Gather our food and points for you to travel
and leave before events here may unravel.
We have surely known you to bear the mark
of the one who could now harness the spark."

FARRU

"Instead, follow the Land 'til it turns right.
Cross the Sun while it is still in your sight.
In eight full moons, you will spy a new place
in a sun-kissed free Tuscan open space."

ANCHISES

"Look for the acts that are certainly wise,
and as sure as the Sun does set and rise.
May your trip begin as well as it can
and end better than even you did plan."

CHAPTER FIVE

HYPERBOLEUM

Cor starts his epic tale after the feast.
A trek is afoot from west to east.
His path impacts Provence to the Levant
and challenges both student and savant.

HYPERBOLEUM

Are the steps we see the ones that he took,
or those that fill the pages of this book?
Does Cor even exist but for our need
to impose our view to support some creed?

HYPERBOLEUM

From afar we see what we want to see,
but that does not mean he ceases to be.
It does not tell us how he sees himself,
or how his tribe labors far below our shelf.

HYPERBOLEUM

Does that mean what he is doing is right
whether it leads to peace or to a fight?
Can we complain if his motives are bad
or if his goals make us happy or sad?

HYPERBOLEUM

We see through more than the lens of an eye,
but blood is blood and salt may make one cry.
It is not relative or just the same.
Wrong is not right due to fortune or fame.

Cor Travels Along the Maritime Border
of Southern France, Stops in a Cave Outside Marseille and then
Turns Right (South) into Italy

NARRATOR

Cor found a path that led to the Great Sea
and a long line to hold so he could soon be
in a plain where the answer could be found
to the question which so shook the ground.

NARRATOR

Did each moon go back or so it did seem
that each step was a drag like a ox team
tied to his full waist to pull him back home
and not to ponder, think or maybe roam?

NARRATOR

He looked left and then to his own right
for the course of the rock to give him sight
and know it was time to turn to the south
for a drink for the mind and a dry mouth.

NARRATOR

Cor felt that there had to be some firm hand
in play with each step on stone rock or sand
or else he would lose his mind from this point
and fall apart limb from limb, joint from joint.

NARRATOR

The Mistral moved in on time and on cue
as if set in time by a skein and clue
that there was an end even at his pace
and that this was a journey, not a race.

27

NARRATOR

Cor took each step, but he did not then know
that Volpe was tracking him high and low.
The shaman thought that Cor should have to die,
as Cor may find where the answers did lie.

NARRATOR

When Cor left and went on this narrow path,
Volpe's blood ran hot fueled by his wrath
and a vow to do what had to be done:
to do right by all means under the Sun.

NARRATOR

The road did rise as the Rhone then did roar;
this river coaxed the last geese to soar.
The delta spoke of no fowl or wild bird
left to guide Cor to his end with a word.

NARRATOR

Cor waded even tho' there were no bridge
across the water to find the stone ridge.
A rock or two from up top hit his head.
Cor fell in a hole, as if he were dead.

NARRATOR

He did not die, but he hurt just the same
then he saw her and he asked her name.
He asked what cave this could be so deep?
What secret she had alone there to keep.

DEB

"My name is Deb she said with her own smirk
You are lucky I was here with my work
to paint the missing prey on the rock wall.
So, I was here to tend to your full fall."

COR

"Do you heal with the touch of your left hand
that applies the herbs and plants on demand
and that draws why the prey you once did eat
no longer are there for our clothes and meat?"

DEB

"I give you some soup made from local oil;
with garlic, saffron and fish on the boil.
Smell the scent of some herbs that I have found
They will tie you to rocks and to the ground."

COR

"Should I not fear one who brings now a gift
which is said to be a salve to uplift,
but which could make me a slave to your taste
and lay my trip and plan to utter waste?"

DEB

"My breast is as supple as your meal full.
They both join to tempt, to tell and to pull.
I sit in silence alone in the caves
Where none can hear above the crash of waves."

29

COR

"I laugh that you act if I will hold you
when it is I who holds the flower true.
You do not live here, but you come to draw
in ash and black the scenes of life so raw."

DEB

"For me, the spirit seal swam with no fear
and led me to this empty dark cave here
to recall the Auk before the ice flow
and the horse and ox we knew long ago."

NARRATOR

With a smile, Deb took the ash in her hand
and made a cross on his head for the land
and a fish on his heart for the Great Sea.
She could only hope he knew what would be.

NARRATOR

Cor fell to sleep, but his eyes did not close.
He stood up like a puffin set to pose
in the new Sun when it comes up so bright
and bids farewell to the passing night.

NARRATOR

A ray of light came from the old flower
to cover the cave in a soft shower
bright from an open door and open room
and from a noiseless, yet still so loud boom.

NARRATOR

Deb did not know how or what she then saw.
There was Charlotte, Mary and coded law.
Clay tablets align each notch for the Moon.
A east trip to where the Sun will rise soon.

NARRATOR

Deb let her hair drop to her now bare back.
She took some oil from out of her own pack
and with ochre and ash she made a sign
of a compass and square level design.

NARRATOR

A fire spark was in the air so she drew
and she drew to call herds old and new
as they went right to intersect the Sun
this is the trip that Cor must now get done.

NARRATOR

Deb then fell to sleep rolled in a ball
like the mare and foal she drew on her wall.
She protected Cor like he was her child
They both slept in tandem so meek and mild.

NARRATOR

A glare on a mist kiss opens his stare,
as he finds that there is no one else there.
He is outside the cave on the road alone,
but he knows he must go down the smooth stone.

NARRATOR

Cor stood and knew he had to walk due east;
he was flush from his fall and from his feast.
He thought he was below only one day,
but two full Moon cycles had made their way.

NARRATOR

At the same time, Volpe was almost home;
his task secure that Cor would not now roam
from that cave and find the answer he sought.
Volpe had won the fight his firm faith fought.

NARRATOR

Cor went on a pace slowly there to mock
his resolve up and down the cold, grey rock.
If a mare bears pain to survive a foal,
surely he could bear less to reach his goal.

NARRATOR

Volpe felt no pain even though each leg hurt.
He had been strong with acute plans so curt.
He did block that new idea so bold —
that Cor may know who called in the cold.

NARRATOR

Cor saw the right turn as the Sun did show
the bend to follow to find each new row
of prey to hunt and to skin all this day,
but like before the herds still were away.

NARRATOR

> Cor knew that there had to be soon some end,
> yet he pauses when he finds this great bend.
> Each sight line sees a path and step so far
> to meet the dusk before the Morning Star.

NARRATOR

> Cor does not fear still to do the same thing
> over and over again, like a ring
> has no beginning and has no seen end.
> Time herds Cor like a single flock to tend.

NARRATOR

> Cor walks slow then fast, then a frantic pace:
> speed and Cor cannot be in the same place.
> Sweat soaks his broad brow from heat on stone,
> as he moves down the path quick, but alone.

NARRATOR

> The road was narrow and then it was wide
> and there before him on the other side
> beyond the gate where lions once did roam
> until ice emerged and covered the loam.

NARRATOR

> There before him was the golden Tuscan plain
> all decked out in the Sun and green main.
> Like the scene the ibex before did show
> to Cor in the cave of life left to sow.

CHAPTER SIX

MARY

"I do not want to have to stop this tale,
as we now have found verdant hill and dell.
Charlotte needs to visit a school or two
to follow her path in the bookish pew."

CHARLOTTE

"Is there a way we can make this go fast
so the end is big and will forever last?
We had a cat that talks and a flower glow,
so let us find the moral we should know."

HYPERBOLEUM

"Cor can only walk as fast as he can do
and allow us to know why certain few
steps and ideas long ago cast the die
of the road and path along which we lie."

DELERIUM

"The past is slow and it serves to reveal
the why and the what of that we conceal.
To know the end without knowing the path
will mimic the pain of the final wrath."

MARY

"Charlotte will long serve and be able to teach
the grasp of her firm mind is the long reach
of a hand that looks for what is not there
and places a new book on a desk bare."

Cor Meets Sica
(It is Not Just Another Boy Meets Girl Story or Maybe it is)

NARRATOR

The land had it own bushes and hedges
in a shape and line along some ledges.
The shape of a horse and a dog in green
was one thing Cor before had never seen.

NARRATOR

Are these the herds that the dream foretold
would return in rows long before the cold.
He cannot feed his tribe on such few plants.
This answer will not feed pangs or old rants.

NARRATOR

Then the Sun did embrace in the late heat
a women with hair sleek like emmer wheat
and pulled back tight with delicate care
in rest on a tunic and nape so bare.

NARRATOR

Cor had a hand to brush away some bees
nestled next to him in a nook of trees.
He did not speak, he just saw the three shapes
of a young woman, a teen and some grapes.

NARRATOR

Sica had a staff as long as the spear
Cor had with him to hunt the ibex and deer.
She was taller than the staff, as was Cor,
and elegant like when a bird does soar.

NARRATOR

Sica knelt down with a plant in the dirt,
Cor saw her lean legs and a blue tartan shirt.
Her hawk eye was on each firm water drop
and each seed in soil to make the new crop.

NARRATOR AND SICA

Sica then spoke to her sister and said,
"the soil seems still and even looks dead,
but mark how seed and stars on my clay pot
rewind and return to this same full spot."

NARRATOR AND ANA

Ana said, "I do not know how seeds tell
when a plant would grow or a crop be well.
I believe a clay goddess figure would,
with oil in the ground, make the crop so good."

NARRATOR AND SICA

With a smile, Sica took Ana's right hand,
"let your eye tell you now to understand.
A stone does not ask the wheat seed to sprout,
but pollen and bees do without a doubt."

NARRATOR AND SICA

Sica lamented and said, "my dear child,
each sign is bold that each hand that is wild
will wilt in the cold and no crops will grow.
So, I must learn why and so I must go."

NARRATOR

Cor was in a spot that was out of sight.
He was up wind a little to their right.
He did not hear each of the spoken words
He hid next to an empty nest for birds.

NARRATOR

He could not take his eye off of her hand.
How her stick did cut and caress the land.
She did drop a seed as a plant should do
in a row with a mist like the early dew.

NARRATOR

She was a dance languid and lean in place.
Her leg and arm was a mime of the pace
of sky, dirt, water and seed set to ask
each bee for his pollen for this one task.

NARRATOR

She made Ana dry her tear to read the soil
and mark the point of the Sun's daily toil.
We do not dance for fun but to grow food
each new cycle we mark in stone and wood.

SICA

"You must know what to do after the cold
retreats and succumbs to golden rays bold.
Do not forget, your tribe will look to you
some day again when the sky is so blue."

NARRATOR

Cor heard a low purr before the crisp crack
of a twig raised the hair along his back.
To his left, right and center was a growl
so deep that it would scare even an owl.

NARRATOR

There were ten lynx cats all in a line
paw to paw and red-orange coats so fine.
The line only made a path to the west
to an end for all which would be the best.

NARRATOR AND SICA

The silence was broken by this sharp sound,
even busy Sica had to turn around.
She said, "Who comes with an army of cats
to a land where there are no mice or rats?"

NARRATOR AND COR

Cor stood up and said with no lasting pride,
"I have come a long way from the far side.
I must take this flower home for the dawn
to see again the game that is now gone."

NARRATOR AND SICA

Sica let out a gasp and said, "I too
have such a plant for which I have no clue.
These cats tell us by their paws and duty:
We go to Cyrnos, the Isle of Beauty."

CYRENE

"We call this council to vote on whether
Sica should leave during this strange weather.
She has been misled by a foreign man
Who deems to hurt us a soon as he can."

SICA

"You are our leader, but our minds tell all
to read and to watch what the facts do call.
No man has sway in lieu of what is true.
I will leave as it is what I must do."

CYRENE

"Your mind is in your new breast and firm thigh.
I too felt lust and the peace and the high.
You shall not leave. Go back now to your field.
I forbid thoughts except the next crop yield."

THE COUNCIL IN UNISON OTHER THAN CYRENE

"There will be a vote and not just one word.
We each can speak and not act like a herd.
The vote is in and Sica shall leave now.
Let us find luck and sacrifice a cow.

CYRENE

"You fools need guidance and not more bold talk.
We shall die if we allow her to walk.
There will come a time when revenge is near.
Sica will suffer so walk now in fear."

41

CHAPTER SEVEN

HYPERBOLEUM

"Mary, you saw the birth of something near.
No, it was not when Cor met Sica here.
The first crop you see was found in one place,
here, then, there and at a very slow pace."

DELERIUM

"When you cull seeds from the chaff, seeds do fall
and Sica's eye would watch the surface wall
of loam erupt in young plants she planted
with life that she, not a silent hand, granted."

HYPERBOLEUM

"There were rows in line with the Sun and rain
and a shed to store and give out the grain.
Spots to join as one by an erect stone
to eat, pray, love, think and not dance alone."

DELERIUM

"One stone led to two stones so on and on
until walls, a city and clothes we don.
But, back to our pair who are long away
from a boat, the wind and the sea spray."

HYPERBOLEUM

"They must deal with Tyrrhenus the sea lord
of the four winds who will not let onboard
one who cannot answer his one riddle
for a passage front, back or middle.

44

Cor and Sica Walk to the Coast to Earn a Boat
From Tyrrhenus, the Sea Lord of the Four Winds, Who Controls All Boats that Float
Off the Tuscan Coast, and Steer to Cyrnos

NARRATOR

Cor could pack for a hunt or a long walk.
He had his bag of points, drink, food and chalk.
But, now he was set and warm to the core.
Sica could pack unlike any before.

NARRATOR

There was a skin for wheat and one for meat
and one for water kept now from the heat.
She had her pots with marks in a row
and burins, shells, and a needles to sow.

NARRATOR

At early light they set off for the Sea.
They spoke of the trails that were soon to be.
Sica knew him like she knew him from birth,
when to be strong or when to feel mirth.

NARRATOR

Sica sought to hear about each cut bone
which had a notch in the shape of a cone
of each phase of the Moon and why the prey
have left before the brisk cold held its sway.

NARRATOR AND TYRRHENUS

They did not feel time or hurt on this walk
so long as each had a chance then to talk.
They would have been swept under a cold Sea
had not a voice said, "Halt now, look at me!"

TYRRHENUS

"I am Old Tyrrhenus, this is My Sea.
The Four Winds listen now only to me.
You may think that I do bluster and gloat,
but without my wind you will have no boat."

TYRRHENUS

"A coin may work to ferry down the Styx,
but no bribe or fee raises a wind to mix
water with sweat as you cross the blue tide
to find what you seek on the other side."

TYRRHENUS

"You both truly seek fair Caillisto's shore
A wave may tempt, yet it is still a door
which will not be open but for the few
who can answer my question posed to you."

TYRRHENUS

"A hundred have tried, and each has now lost.
Pride will shrink from the fear and the true cost.
You may boast, but you will be next to fail.
Surely, a hundred and two will not sail."

TYRRHENUS

"No woman has tried, so I like the test.
Man or woman, I will remain the best.
So which one of you will be my next foe
and leave in a lurch with a heart of woe."

COR

"The wind did howl and laugh as if to say
that it does not fear that today is the day
that it may have to work to push the boat
and keep the bow upright and still afloat."

NARRATOR AND SICA

Sica stood calming the firm blowing wind.
She did not falter and she did not bend.
"If I do not win, but let me now try.
I will surely fall to your barbs so wry!"

SICA

"Tell me the riddle that is hoary old
that shifts like the sand and the sea so bold.
I will see if I know what the words mean
and if I can find an answer to glean."

TYRRHENUS

"You try to entice me to tell some clues.
You feign to be slow, but that is a ruse.
You must have more than wits and some old sight
to answer: Good accounts make what tonight?"

SICA

"You want me to say chert, wealth and gold
or the return of the herds would be bold.
The arc of this riddle is what never bends:
Good accounts, I know, make very good friends."

NARRATOR

The old man gasps hard, as Sica is right,
but she could still be a loser if she might
not know the hidden moral of this tale
and thus Cor and Sica still could not set sail.

TYRRHENUS

"You are the first one, but you are not done.
You read the wry words, but you have not won.
What is the lesson to give to your tribe
if you say these lean words as a new scribe?"

SICA

"The words are so firm and mean what they say.
They mean the same yesterday and today.
They apply to all and that is a key.
This is advice that I would give for free."

TYRRHENUS

"You have told me nothing but empty words
that may make sharp noise to confound the birds.
Auks are noisy birds, but they do not fly;
this is your rare second and final try "

SICA

"If I give you a staff, points and a core
I do not expect the same gift or more.
Yet, the balance of the account is now square;
I have more then to cherish and to share."

48

NARRATOR

Tyrrhenus sighs and gives Sica a goat.
He then presents to her a stunning coat
with flowing purple trim and simple shells
of spirals that once were below the swells.

NARRATOR

At the dock moors the prize of her new boat.
Beech bark mixes with tar so it will float.
A stout deck extends as long as four men.
It sits wide in the Sea like a flat bin.

NARRATOR

Below deck are jars of recently cut wheat,
fish, goat, peas, chestnut, salt, and figs so sweat.
There are large clay pots with embers and soot.
There was mint, basil, peas and ginger-root.

NARRATOR

The firm rudder waits with an open sail.
A wood cabin embraces new tales to tell.
Plush down cushions lie for Sica to dream
in the current of the waves or music stream.

NARRATOR

She finds this bed, closing her tired eyes,
Cor takes the rudder without any sighs.
He steers the boat headlong into the spray.
The Four Winds howl and guide all of the way.

NARRATOR

She dreams, but she is awake in the boat.
She is bare and alone on foam afloat.
She stands straight in the core of a sea shell
Glistening and glowing in the mist swell.

NARRATOR

Her brown hair unfolds and flow like a sash
to cover her gracile form with a dash
of flair and grace blushing in the new light
of the Sun shining near to her so bright.

NARRATOR AND BILK

Before her stands Bilk the Quinotaur there,
"I can form that shape you want or so dare.
Do you want a bull, a swan, or god wild?
What do you want since you were a child?"

BILK

"I live in the Sea in both future and past;
my seed will spawn a line that will long last.
Will it start now or wait for a new lode?
Do I have to keep talking in this code?"

NARRATOR AND SICA

She stayed pure and did not miss a beat,
"You tempt and try to knock me off the seat
that holds me safe and firm to this grand chore.
I have but one choice, and he, is my core."

NARRATOR

She awakes to the sound of the storm surge,
Without doubt, she follows some rising urge
to be with Cor while the waves hit the side
and he does not move or shrink with such pride.

COR

"I wish I could always steady the line
as you feel the sleep and your dreams so fine.
You are my soul and rock on sea or ground;
my life-line now in this storm-driven sound."

NARRATOR AND SICA

She did not often say what her heart felt,
"I did sleep and feel how the fear did melt.
You enter my heart and make me complete.
No idea, no goal, no man can compete."

NARRATOR

The coast was well within their joint sight.
The boat was direct tacking left than right.
He was drawn by a small still half-moon cove.
He had stumbled upon a treasure trove.

COR

"I still do not know what will be the name
of this great gift, that like you, is not tame,
but with you it is the source of my life
where there will be no fulsome fear or strife."

NARRATOR

The clear blue marina accepted the pair.
The surface was still with no wind out there.
She could see herself and the life below.
A cold stone beach spread like a curved bow.

NARRATOR

Cor landed the full boat firm on the land
and set the anchor and rope with his hand
around a trim trunk of an old oak tree
that was the gate to the limbs near the sea.

NARRATOR

They would soon observe a second full moon.
The food stock was full and would not end soon.
He would find the trail in the trees and deer
and she would find a place to plant so near.

NARRATOR

Should they start now, he did muse and say
when she ran up and showed the short way
to play with the dolphin, otter and fish
and do now what they want and what they wish.

NARRATOR

They found each other in the salt and spray
and when she went back to the boat that day.
She sat up under her coat of bear fur,
as he fed mussels, figs and oats to her.

NARRATOR

They were both worn out without much to say,
yet her touch and his pulse made the way
for them to pose stout and straight like an owl
as they slept as one like cuddling fowl

NARRATOR

But, it was then during the black of the night
that Bilk the Quinotaur came from out of sight
and stole onto the boat for each flower
hoping to capture her with their power.

NARRATOR

Bilk found the flowers, but without the key
to tap the power that would be let free.
Bilk knew a shaman who could help him now.
Bilk had to find the man with just one cow.

NARRATOR

From the boat, Bilk went on the path he laid
'til he had to find out what fate had made.
Bilk put each flower down on the cold path
and felt the cold grasp of unbroken wrath.

NARRATOR

One plant was a lynx, the other a ram
with a growl and grunt set Bilk on the lam.
The lynx would serve Sica, as it could.
The ram would help Cor, as only it should.

Narrator

Sica left the boat at the crack of dawn.
She saw a lynx in the trees with a fawn.
The cat put her paw in the air to show
Sica the open path for her to go.

Narrator

The forest hid the mountain's violent past
of the thrust of hot rocks that would long last
to form the flat terrace and the firm ground
still moving on its own without any sound.

Narrator

It took Sica half the Sun's path to find
the way through the trees and every kind
of plant and stone that made the journey long
even when she sang her favorite song.

Narrator

She found the terrace and each eye was set
to find each new plant and new seed still wet
from the misty dew which set up in pools
and fed each flower and plant with no tools.

Narrator

With her staff, she drew each new line to sow
after which she would watch that seed then grow.
She could now feed more than she ever knew,
when she found on the ground her flower too.

NARRATOR

Cor saw that Sica had left, so he sat
on the bow of the boat on a reed mat.
It was then an old mouflon's boastful yell
made him jump up to the hunt without fail.

NARRATOR

Cor did not know where to go, but each male
would follow a curve along the bent trail
to take Cor away from his lamb and ewe
to find a spot where he could head-butt you.

NARRATOR

Can Cor out-flank and out-pace his new prey?
What a feast he would make later this day.
He made his own circle up wind and fast.
There was no way for this old ram to last.

NARRATOR

Cor found his spot within range of his spear.
The ram could sense him, but it did not fear.
He shut each eye before he made his throw,
but the ram was gone before he did know.

NARRATOR

Cor saw the place where the ram did not cower
and found, by himself, his own true flower.
Behind a tree were the signs of the herds
of auruch, ibex and tasty small birds.

55

NARRATOR

They each went home in the early moonlight.
They both could not wait to tell of each sight
they saw that day and why they should now stay
where the plants grow and there is many prey.

NARRATOR

The answer they sought was within their grasp
and they would no longer feel the cold rasp
of the ice that cracks the stone and the seed.
Both of their tribes would have all that they need.

NARRATOR

They were hungry, but who could stop and eat
or hug or kiss when they each had to meet
to speak of things more than the cave did tell
and would write the facts of a brand new tale.

COR

"I saw the signs of the herds that were lost
that could feed the whole tribe at little cost.
If I mark the land and I cull the prey,
I will soon call my group to find the way."

SICA

"I have the place where food will grow for all.
The Sun shows me if the rows rise or fall.
My hand will till the moist dirt and brown moss
and my people will not be at a loss."

56

NARRATOR

Cor and Sica spoke well into the night
as a star did dance near the Moon so bright.
It was time to hunt game, but not to sow.
She could cure meat with no seeds to grow.

NARRATOR

Would it now be time for them to leave soon
so they could be back before the new Moon?
There were answers to tell first to her clan
of hunts and herds and later of her plan.

NARRATOR

They then fell asleep to muse and to dream
and slept till the Sun rose above the stream.
Cor arose to see a boat with full sail
head to him on a fast pace without fail.

NARRATOR AND FARRU

Cor spoke to Sica to pick up his spear
and join him now to allay any fear.
"As a conch turns, you now are my sole host
and it is I, not you, that needs food most."

NARRATOR AND FARRU

Farru then stood up speaking to his friend.
"I really do not seek a wound to mend.
Just a fire, a bed and food to eat.
May I land and see if there is some meat?"

NARRATOR

Cor fell as he sought to steady the boat
and as Sica brought out an herb cured goat.
Farru bent down and held out his old hand
and soon he was with Cor on the dry land.

NARRATOR AND FARRU

Farru ate and drank as if he did race
his words to confirm the fear in his face.
"The Massif is seized by sheets of ice
as is the Tuscan plain not once but twice."

FARRU

"Each clan is safe, but there is no way home.
There is no warm place for us now to roam.
I am dying so thanks, but I must go
to reach the Sunset along with the crow."

NARRATOR

Cor put Farru in his boat with a coat
and cast him adrift alone then to float.
Sica put a spark to tar in the pot
and it caught fire and sank on the spot.

NARRATOR

Sica went to the beach to find a shell
to give to the Sea and thereby to tell
Farru that he did what he had to do
and that he lived a life that was true.

Narrator and Sica

She then put the sea shell on its own way,
and with it, she had few firm words to say,
"we walk, we talk, and we plant and we build,
and it is by these acts we make our yield."

Narrator

They next went to the cabin and laid down
He closed his eyes and she did not frown.
Alone, he held her and she held him tight.
Up was now down and left was now right.

Narrator

Each of their flowers fell onto the floor,
the lynx and the ram then guarded the door.
The Moon lifted higher into the night
A Moon shadow kept the boat out of sight.

Narrator

Cor and Sica made a strong body whole.
They were now forever body and soul.
Their bond with the land could never be torn.
This is how Corsica, the Isle, was born.

CHAPTER EIGHT

Entre'Act
Hyperboleum, Delerium, Mary and Charlotte
Provide Some Perspective

MARY

"This is not the end of the translation.
The text speaks of more than just a nation.
Is it that the words may just be a bore,
or is there still the seed for life and lore?"

CHARLOTTE

"My mom is right about the words and text.
The tale twists, tugs and turns until the next
tablet unveils the story of three twins
who see the global axis while it spins."

HYPERBOLEUM

"Does a minute last only a short time?
Why do you rush the measure of the rime?
Does a flower start without its own seed?
Why not pause to listen to what we read?"

DELERIUM

"Cor and Sica gave us three sets of sons
born of each pain and stratum that still runs
from the Sea to each free mountain pass
as truly as bronze comes from zinc and brass."

HYPERBOLEUM

"For thirty years, they hunted and grew food
guiding the hearts and mind of their brood.
When hope and right became their blood and bone
They died in peace and left their sons alone."

62

Gallus and Albion
(the Original Celtic Gauls and Britons)

NARRATOR

Gallus and Albion were the oldest.
They were the first to act and the boldest.
Each had the same nose, gait, gesture and hair.
They were the same, an identical pair.

NARRATOR

At first they would hunt and play together.
One tandem alike in any weather.
Gallus was the first to tame all new mares.
Albion could entice bears from their lairs.

NARRATOR

When it was time for each to walk about;
they left without fear or without doubt.
They would be apart, but always be bound.
They had a pact forged from the firm ground.

NARRATOR

Albion marked the curved Sun's arc
to where the land sank alone into the dark
along with the North Star to the world's edge
to where there was a chalky mountain ledge.

NARRATOR

The Sea's arc was the line that Gallus took.
North then west to each stream, river and brook.
From the peaks in the east and the coast line
to the plains with grain and herds of fine kine.

63

Acheus and Remus
(the Original Greeks and Romans)

NARRATOR

Acheus was the next son to be born
Remus then came, so Cor blew a loud horn.
They were similar, but different though.
Remus would reap what Acheus would sow.

NARRATOR

Acheus left first by ship to the coast
seeking to out-flank the Sun with no boast.
He went down, left, up and then around
until the plain of Argos was then found.

NARRATOR

Soon, a lion-gate capped a high stone wall
with an oval bee-hive chamber so tall
in which he put all of the recent grain
from each tribe on or near his fertile plain

NARRATOR

Remus could not sit and stay still at rest.
He sought to find his brother as his test.
He could learn as he did and as he grew,
'til it was time for him to start anew.

NARRATOR

Remus went out, but his path was cut short
by a she-wolf and geese at a marsh port
that fed a river and seven hills home
from where he would not ever again roam.

Catalanus and Hispanus
(the Original Catalans and Spanish)

NARRATOR

The last sons were strangers to each other,
as if they did not have the same mother.
They will deny each other's fame or name,
yet it is true their parents were the same.

NARRATOR

Catalanus went to find Cor's old home,
and set sail alone among the Sea foam.
He made land where his father had begun;
it was now with the bulls he sought to run.

NARRATOR

He ran in the hills and through the steep pass
by the mountain ice and sharp crevasse
'til he found the Ebro and the Sea line;
set to hunt the prey upon which to dine.

NARRATOR

Hispanus went on his own path by boat.
He set no course himself except to float
if the wind may now take him each new day.
He could talk to himself with much to say.

NARRATOR

The wind did its part and found the land fall.
He set forth to find food and a new hall.
His wish was met on a Castilian plain.
Where he decided he would then remain.

65

Volpe Made a Pact with Goth the Dragon
When His Trip from the South is Cut Short
By the Onset of the Younger Dryas

NARRATOR

Volpe was cut short by the ice and snow.
If he would then make it, he did not know.
So, he found a cave to sit through the night.
He did not think he was up for a fight.

NARRATOR AND GOTH

Did he shake from the cold or from each word
that met him and sent a chill when he heard,
"Do I eat you now or just have some fun.
the fire in my mouth is like the Sun."

VOLPE

"O great dragon, I am not a worthwhile meal.
You would prefer an auruch or a seal.
I am an old shaman with only bones
that rattle to scare and creak with my moans."

GOTH

"I do not see an ox, a fox or deer.
It is just you and me and that is clear.
I have not eaten food for some time now.
You will do just fine, as there is no cow."

NARRATOR

Volpe took a charm and made it soon fall
while he made like a mad black badger ball.
A mist and breath felt his nape and his hand,
as he was set to die now in the sand.

66

NARRATOR

But wait, there was no roar and just a sigh
as the dragon laid back and did not try
to eat Volpe or conjure up a flame.
The beast was sick, tired and very lame.

GOTH

"I have no teeth and this is my own cell.
My sentence for my past sins in the tale
of where each tooth became a man with fire
to form an army of hate for long hire."

VOLPE

"You are Goth from the land of the cold bear
out of time and place in this dry cave lair.
I can help you re-grow your teeth and might
and again we can create such a fright."

VOLPE

"My eyes burn with the fire you have lost
I want to destroy Cor at any cost.
Feel the heat from the red rock that rumbles
to heal you 'til the sky lifts and tumbles."

NARRATOR

Volpe and Goth made a pact and blood oath.
Herbs and hate mark the moons 'til they both
were fit to start the cruel war to be won
and waged now against Cor and each son.

NARRATOR

Volpe had envy and he could not rest
as long as Cor and Sica beat the test.
He bit a bird when he heard they were dead.
Their children must slowly die in their stead.

VOLPE

"We will defeat Albion in his white hill
who will call for Gallus whom we will kill.
The rest are too young to offer a fight.
They will all withdraw once we are in sight."

NARRATOR

One thousand teeth became soldiers for hire.
Each man had an axe, a short spear and fire.
They came by small boats of both sail and oar;
all safely arrived on Albion's shore.

NARRATOR

The warriors formed a single-file snake
of fire that began to raze or take
all land, crops and villages in their path
which witnessed a weary wake of wrath.

NARRATOR

Albion sped to attack with no fear;
His men spread out in a tight human weir.
The snake line stalled, stuck unable to move.
Fifteen full moons saw them set in a grove.

NARRATOR

Brutus was sent to Gallus to find aid
to be put on new boats with white sails made
of flax with a red cross to show the tie
that bound brothers until they would both die.

NARRATOR

Gallus had to stay to place men and wood
to defend his home and band if there should
be war while he and his men were away
so there would be an army for the fray.

NARRATOR

The sky then was black with a sheen so bright
like an obsidian point in fire light.
It was Goth reborn with smoke and with flair
as he landed from his flight in the air.

GOTH

"The land of your brother knows of my kind,
as we may be sent far and wide to find
the Sun that gets lost in the mist so deep
that engulfs all before the Sun may leap."

GOTH

"I will take you across the channel wide
So you may be at your brother's side.
Come with me now there is no time to wait.
We will soon both test what is your true fate."

NARRATOR

With a flap and crack and no time to spare
Gallus found a perch high in the cold air.
He soon saw a fire line that was stuck
like an ibex which jumped in the muck.

NARRATOR

With a lurch and drop, Goth twisted right.
Gallus pulled hard, but he could not fight
the hand of the wave from the dragon's tail
that pushed and poked until he fell.

GOTH

"I know your fate, of that I did not lie.
Now, Albion will see you fall and die.
Volpe will get the gift that he deserves.
There will be no help from any reserves."

NARRATOR

Gallus fell fast with a grasp for the sky
lost in a turn and twist in air so high.
Fast and furious he went down and down
A rock below now would be his sure crown.

NARRATOR

When just as fast, there was a golden head
that broke his fast fall before he was dead.
He sat on the back of a beast so sleek -
it made Goth look flimsy, wanton and weak.

TOM

"I am Tom and I bear many a scar
from the talon of Goth both near and far,
but my light inside once before did save
me as I fought and put him in a cave."

NARRATOR

In a swoop, Tom left Gallus on the ground
next to his bold brother whom he soon found
set to cut the fire-snake apart in two
along a firm line the white chalk did drew.

NARRATOR

Tom split the sky to seek out his old foe.
Goth did not wait and from his mouth did blow
a spray to blind Tom and to make him crash.
Goth spew forth bile and cut Tom with a gash.

NARRATOR

The blood was warm, but did not slow Tom down.
He set forth to a spot below Goth's frown.
Goth buckled with the pierce of a close claw
and fell so fast hurling from his wound raw.

NARRATOR

Goth then sought to regroup to strike once more,
but Tom's aim was true and hit to the core.
A single short swipe cut Goth up in two
and Goth became dust that spread in the blue.

NARRATOR

The fire-snake went south and to the north-east.
It had no care of the death of the beast.
Albion let the top half leave and run.
He chose to fight the low half under the Sun.

NARRATOR

His foe slinked off through hill and dry glen.
It went to find help in the land of tin
where the Sun sets each day before the pall
and set up a line behind a corn wall.

NARRATOR

They fought very close with breath in each face.
'Til each slash could not keep up with the pace
of death on each side whose ranks became thin.
Albion would prevail, but did not win.

NARRATOR

The fight had been close and the point was made
as the fight went on and the day did fade.
A spear-point flew fast at Albion's back,
but Gallus was there to meet the attack.

NARRATOR

The brothers embraced and marked the day
to build a fire and a new home to stay.
This Tintangle will show what happened here
when truth was fair and beat down hearts of fear.

CHAPTER NINE

(Charlotte, Mary, Hyperboleum, and Delerium
Discuss Plot Technique and Introduce the Last Chapter)

CHARLOTTE

"Why did dragons have to be in the plot?
They fly, fight, figure, fuss and talk a lot.
Why did the cat and ibex fail to show?
Why not a fearsome fox or boastful crow?"

HYPERBOLEUM

"Why do you ask about the dragon lore?
It fills great texts, tales and stories galore.
From east to west and then from north to south
writ down for ages or by word of mouth."

DELERIUM

"You should ask about the half-snake that left.
It is set to strike at and set to cleft.
It targets the brothers and family bond.
Blood will soak soil and many a pond."

HYPERBOLEUM

"The half-snake again became whole as one
seeking to win what once could not be won.
Each son of Cor would see fire then soar,
as life went on as the world was at war."

MARY

"The world at war is what now peaks our mind.
The fabric of life feels for ties that bind.
The smell of death sifts from this oldest tale.
There must be a hero found without fail."

74

The Marina of Meria Where Cor and Sica
First Landed

NARRATOR

Meria awakes with bursting Sun light
A sense of firm hands marks the dawn's long fight
to seize spirals, shells and mussels that might
lure a man to sail into rays so bright.

NARRATOR

Paths cut like veins through the oaks and pines
and spread out on the mountain side like tines
of a chalk deer alive in a stone prance
seizing the heart and mind in a cold trance.

NARRATOR

This is war and sails open in a race
to unfurl and move ahead of the pace
of the pall of death that turns the face pale
and tears the fiber and soul without fail.

NARRATOR

A sentry fire sends smoke to each home
when it is safe to leave and when to roam.
A store of food is tall with shocks of wheat
to be ground and mixed with fresh rare meat.

NARRATOR

The village pulsed like ants in a pile
that had been kicked over for awhile.
Each knew their own job in this fluid race
to defend each hearth and hope in this space.

75

NARRATOR

In the swirl of defense, Babu is cool
and he does not move save to watch the pool
of dew on a rock where wheat chaff was shorn
only a few steps from where he was born.

NARRATOR

He stood tall above his longest straight spear.
No hand or horn may spark the flame of fear.
He was still, not being one set to talk,
but waiting on the path that she would walk.

NARRATOR

Ursu was as tall as him, but was lean
yet strong. She could not be rash, weak or mean.
She came from the land of hops and small bears
As one, they each had no known fears or cares.

NARRATOR

He could hear her talk of a tale of strife
but with such hope and a love of all life.
She was his spirit for his soul each year
Her smirk and smile did wipe away each tear.

NARRATOR

She could watch him toil and work in time.
His touch felt firm and his song was a chime
to call her heart and mind to meet the beat
of the measure where there is no defeat.

NARRATOR

But it was Bumpu that came up the path
who spoke of the war and the blood and wrath.
Bumpu was blank and shorter than a spear,
yet sharp like an old fox with a young deer.

BUMPU

"How can you be here waiting just for her
when she is not a dream, but a cold cur
with a spell hiding the fate of our clan
as if she has some steadfast thought and plan?"

BABU

"You do not know why she makes me so strong
or why her words tempt my soul to long
for my home free from made-up hurt and fear
and on a path that is lucid and clear."

BUMPU

"I know the grasp of a blind man can feel
each point in a sewn pattern that is real.
Ursu will not come, as she now lies dead.
They killed her as she slept in her bed."

BABU

"How did the kin of Volpe strike this blow?
Did they use an ax, a spear or a long bow?
No, I will not be led by idle words.
She will come, as she has, with the blue birds."

NARRATOR

Babu did wait, as he then had to do.
The Sun rose high as blue birds came and flew.
The nip of dusk arose near the path's end.
No one came and there was no word to send.

NARRATOR

It was time to eat and someone could tell
if she ate or if she stood fast or fell
or if she sold fresh bread or if she bought
the emmer wheat that she needed and sought.

NARRATOR

The fire was hot with talk of the long war.
The talk of her fate did not make new lore.
Babu did not stop asking each one there:
where was Ursu, as if each one did care.

NARRATOR

No one saw her any time that short day.
Two men were seen leaving during a fray
from her house with a cloth over one thing
that did not move, but that did have a ring.

NARRATOR

Babu then left to find her bed to see
if what he did fear had come now to be.
But, a fire did burn to cleanse her house
and he found only ashes and a blouse.

NARRATOR

Babu did not wait to paint his face red.
It was her own shade on pots to bake bread.
He wore an old cloak of blue and off white.
Her colors would still shine during his fight.

NARRATOR

He ran until he slept for a short while.
He arrived with the Sun, as he built a pile
of bones outside to honor his own clan.
He was ready to fight with his own plan.

NARRATOR

He stood in a Sun-spray along with the dew
while the night lost again to something new.
He could end it now if he beat their best
so he made his choice of a boast and geste.

BABU

"Send me one who will fight to win it all
if there is one among you, short or tall,
who can feel the edge of my sharpest point
when I cut you in pieces joint by joint."

ANGELINA

"I accept, as a woman's tongue is sharp.
My moves are fluid like a river carp.
Can you live if a female hand wins out?
Or will you hector, as you die and pout?"

CHAPTER TEN

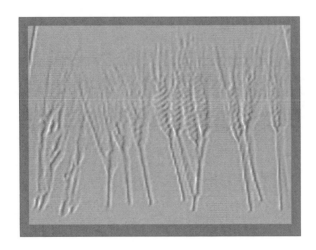

The Roman Quartet: Charlotte Questions
Hyperboleum and Delerium About the Plot
Twist of a Woman Warrior Champion

CHARLOTTE

"Wait, why would a woman fight for the host?
This was a man's world to live in and boast.
This is a modern twist and plot device.
There should be a giant, as my advice."

HYPERBOLEUM

"So, Homer is new to you and not so old
to have an Amazon fight Greeks so bold?
Was Athena's hold on wisdom and war
now just a recent idea for new lore?"

MARY

"I see your point, but who still reads old tales
of the epic role of females and males
in songs, poems, myths, and dusty old stories
or ancient texts, lore, tablets and glories."

DELERIUM

"Well, this is old text writ small in stone
of a distaff warrior strong with spear and bone
who will lose to Babu so all is right,
as we get back to the tale of the fight."

HYPERBOLEUM

"Babu is gracious and spares her own life,
but she will still suffer none else but hard strife
as he too does even when he brings peace.
Yes, he won, but there is no golden fleece."

82

NARRATOR

Babu struck first with a fist to her face.
He then cut her side twice and sought to trace
a path to her spleen with each flaked edge.
He tried to push her against a ledge.

NARRATOR

With a feint and jab, she pierced his left side
The pain was cold and hurt not just his pride.
He fell to a knee and yelled in pain.
A twitch froze his left arm up to his brain.

NARRATOR

Up and down, right and left, over and back
they fought with neither giving any slack.
But when the Sun rose high as it would be,
she fell quickly and her army did flee.

NARRATOR

He stood over her and sang her praises
as the worthy warrior heart who raises
his respect and the right to live once more.
It was time though to settle this new score.

NARRATOR

Volpe's army left fast at a quick pace.
They left leaving almost no wake or trace.
Babu had saved Meria for now,
but Volpe still hoped for them to bow.

NARRATOR

Volpe now met with Cyrene to make new war.
Vengeance bore a hoard evil at its core.
Their number was unknown, but for the mass
of arms that choked each plain, peak and pass.

NARRATOR

The wins by Gallus and Babu gave hope,
but the rings of fire and stone made a rope
so tight that light seemed to fade to dark
with each loss, like a dull mind without spark.

NARRATOR

Tom and Babu then went from place to place
to find the salve of a legion in space
to lead by deeds and be the vanguard host
to rally the attack from coast to coast.

NARRATOR

Dante spoke no words but held the line fast
and split open heads with a precise blast
so Mike could yell and run through with no fear
such that soon there were no heads left to shear.

NARRATOR

Tim shot an arrow so well that the Sun
blushed that its long arc was left undone.
Martin had built the length of the long bow
to fire firm, straight, often, fast and slow.

Narrator

George used wit to beat a larger foe
thirsty from a river with a cut flow.
Craig kept each warrior in a direct line
with food, plans and an overall design.

Narrator

Johnny was the bold heart pulsing them on
with a balm of bravery he would don.
Mike and Mark fought each other as a ruse
so clever their foes never saw their clues.

Narrator

Jim could outrun and outlast any man
with such grace, guile, and gusto as he can.
Rob was as large as any mountain high
and during each fight he held up the sky.

Narrator

Katie was there with her bag-pipes to call
Jo made fine festive food for one and all.
Donna and Denise were each fierce and brave.
Sue was called on more than once to save.

Narrator

David made sure that the war remained just
crafting a fair peace from the ruin and dust.
Pat was the voice that made sense of all things
as the narrator pulling all the strings.

NARRATOR

Many moons came and went on land and sea.
But blood built a bridge over grass now free.
The win came only with many lives lost
They found their goal, but at such a high cost.

NARRATOR

The hero of any war is the one
who comes home when the war is lost or won.
No words can re-make the sacrifice made,
but some heroes will receive a parade.

NARRATOR

Babu came home to stay and without fear.
He found Bumpu hiding like a lost deer
among the crowd who spoke, but did not fight
and who now were heroes of awesome might.

NARRATOR

It was a time not to ask or tarry,
as there were friends to mourn and to bury
and it was hard for those to stay at home
as those who had fought had to leave and roam.

NARRATOR

There was a great fire to burn the dead
and dust would swirl in eddies for a bed.
They could dance in shadows from the fire
as the cold night fought back the great pyre.

The Short-Lived Feast

NARRATOR

There was a feast for Babu and his clan.
It was time for cheer without any plan.
All were so close to hear words from his lips
that they did not hear the docking of ships.

BABU

"I fought to honor my Muse and great love
who went to her death on a path above.
Let us erect this straw before the stone
is set for the statute of her alone."

URSU

"Maybe, I do not look good in steel gray.
I would prefer to have something to say
that you find a cold slab for one who died
with a family which still has cried."

BABU

"What magic is this that you appear now?
How did you cheat cold death making it bow?
What pact did you make to once again stand
among those that dance within the close band?"

URSU

"Did you hit your hard head in a close fight
that you did not know of the trip that night
I took seeking peace in a foreign land
as Bumpu gave me your cloth for my hand."

BABU

"Why I went to war to kill was a lie!
My head was false and others had to die?
I misled death, yet they cheer out my name.
My own heart burns at the end of this game."

BUMPU

"Do not fear now for what you did was good.
I told you she died or else then you would
not have fought well while I was here at home.
Do not ask why the warm blood soaks the loam."

NARRATOR

The crowd sang a chorus of a new song
of Babu the wise and Babu the strong.
The strains were a wave that wiped his brow
and sought to erase the when, who and how!

NARRATOR

But, Babu knew that he had to go east
like Cor did to conquer the gripping beast
in his head in search of an answer true
in a land with two rivers and a clue.

NARRATOR

Ursu too knew his path for the new morn
to find the cure to save a life forlorn.
She may not join him, as he had to find
why he should live in his body or mind.

The Journey East to the Land Between Two Rivers
(or Mesopotamia)

NARRATOR

Ursu and Babu left the cheering crowd.
They stood tall as one while the clan was loud.
She knew that she had to be clear and strong
for both of them even if he were wrong.

NARRATOR

She put her hand on the door to her home,
as he kissed her neck saying he will not roam
when he comes back from his trip to find hope.
He would be happy and would not than mope.

NARRATOR

She sat him down and went to wash her face.
She put on a dress that showed a trace
of each breast and leg while she put on oil
from the lilac to make his cold blood boil.

NARRATOR

She found him with his shirt off and chest bare.
He just sat there looking away to stare
at a clay wall with red hands and a star.
He was both close to her and yet so far.

NARRATOR

He caught her hand to find his lost strength
while she searched hard for some breadth and length.
There was a flower she never had seen
that he held in his hands and heart so lean.

URSU

"What flower do you caress in each hand?
I am strong and firm and can help you stand.
The plant will die in due course and time.
Where did you get it as part of some rime?"

BABU

"A young girl gave it to me after one fight.
She said a talking cat came by one night
and told her to give it to an old man
the next time the wildest dogs of war ran."

URSU

"Yes, cats and ibex may talk, but not now.
I am here to show you when, who and how.
Bumpu may smile, but he could not win.
You have deeds which even he cannot spin."

BABU

"Why does the Moon haunt me when I have you
before me to anchor all that is true?
I smell death and not the lilac you wear.
Have I not won all for which I should care?"

URSU

"You are of an old line that cares too much.
'Why' is your warm heart and 'How' is your touch.
You are the same, as a mouflon is tough
or a shell winds and winds and hides enough."

NARRATOR

Babu then knew that he had indeed won.
He dropped his arm, as Ursu was the one.
They fell the same in a bed warm and lean.
Life now was not pain, but was hope unseen.

NARRATOR

Tom the dragon greeted him at first light
and prepared him for the next bumpy flight
to dance with tall peaks in skies of azure
around dolmens, menhirs and old treasure.

NARRATOR

Gobeckli Tepe was an old stone gate
above the two rivers that did create
a fertile crescent of land with new grain
that could, with peace, grow anew with the rain.

NARRATOR

Stone bird heads frown, but they did not call
to the lions and trees that made a hall
as a circle henge for the flattened mound
with stories and tales, but it made no sound.

NARRATOR

Tom showed Babu marks cut in the wall,
like his antler saw the Moon rise and fall,
and made by a clan at a prior date
with a force of destiny and set fate.

NARRATOR

En-An stood behind the wall from afar.
Inana was closer wearing the star
of the Moon and spiral on her fresh neck
like Babu's that he had from his kin's trek.

BABU

"You and I live the tandem that we wear.
We seek life anew that can have no fear.
Peace abounds when the clans come as one here
to share ideas, art, craft, herbs, wool and deer."

INANA

"That was true before the cold and the flower,
but gaps and cracks spread with each stark shower
of frozen ice and rain to seed the hate
that splits the clans and may just seal our fate."

EN-AN

"Go to our home in Uruk to find hope
and form a plan making us all to cope
as we once did when the stones were cold blanks
and foes did not plot schemes among our flanks."

NARRATOR

Tom flew Babu to Uruk in one day.
Tom built a stone mound for Babu to stay
and to call the clans as once they did hear
the wisdom that forged ties that were clear.

92

NARRATOR

This ziggurat bore the sign of the star
and the spiral that wise men from afar
knew and hoped what had been long foretold --
that a king would come with this sign so bold.

NARRATOR

The clan heads came to the large house now built
with baked bricks formed by hand from silt
of each river bed that fed each war clan
who now were there to hear Babu's new plan.

NARRATOR

Each man could not just eat and sit and talk.
Each had to be closest, as each would walk.
Words even won over deeds lost in the gold
that was so dear and made each so bold.

NARRATOR

Babu did not know what he would then say
to bring, as one, each clan on this new day.
He sought his flower, but it was then dust.
Ursu tough had told him what he should trust.

BABU

"You are blind to the blood and deeds that bind.
You choose not to see, and lust clouds the mind.
You do nor hear, but attack and react.
But, it is time that you all lead by pact."

URSU

"One has copper and the other has tin.
Apart, they are cold and no one will win.
As one, they are bronze to use, plow and build
and grow crops for all from one common field."

BABU

"One knows how to plant, but has no firm will.
The other does, but has no seeds to till.
Apart, all want food and fight out of fear.
As one, there is bread, peas, peace and beer."

NARRATOR

Babu became Lugal and all were one.
Ursu joined him and success was won.
The scribes wrote of deeds on tablets of clay.
Sumer was born and shines until this day.

NARRATOR

Mary opened, "In Kramer we all will read
how the scribes set down and could then succeed
to write on clay tablets of Uruk's speed
to incubate civilization's seed."

94

39281870R00057

Made in the USA
Columbia, SC
09 December 2018